The Best Bear in All the World

EGMONT

We bring stories to life

First published in Great Britain 2016
by Egmont UK Limited
This edition published in 2017 by Egmont UK LImited
The Yellow Building, 1 Nicholas Road, London W11 4AN
www.egmont.co.uk

Stories by Paul Bright, Brian Sibley, Jeanne Willis and Kate Saunders
copyright © 2016 Trustees of the Pooh Properties
Illustrations by Mark Burgess copyright © 2016 Trustees of the Pooh Properties

Illustrations in the Afterword selected from:

Winnie-the-Pooh and *The House at Pooh Corner*
Line illustrations copyright © 1926 and 1928 E.H.Shepard
Colouring of the line illustrations copyright ©
1970 and 1974 E.H.Shepard and Egmont UK Limited

When We Were Very Young and *Now We Are Six*
Line illustrations copyright © 1924 and 1927 E.H.Shepard
Colouring of the line illustrations by Mark Burgess copyright © 1989 Egmont UK Limited

Photograph of A.A.Milne and Christopher Robin by Howard Coster copyright © Apic/Getty Images

Photograph of E.H.Shepard copyright © The Shepard Trust

Photograph of A.A.Milne and Christopher Robin copyright © Culture Club/Getty Images

Edited by Rebecca Oku and Nicole Pearson
Designed by Pritty Ramjee

ISBN 978 1 4052 8661 9
55085/2

Printed in China

A CIP catalogue record for this title is available
from The British Library.

The
Best Bear
in All
the World

*in which we join Winnie-the-Pooh for a year of
adventures in the Hundred Acre Wood*

By
Paul Bright, Brian Sibley, Jeanne Willis and Kate Saunders
based upon the Pooh stories by A.A.Milne
with decorations by Mark Burgess
in the style of E.H.Shepard

EGMONT

EXPOSITION

'Ninety?' said Winnie-the-Pooh. 'Is that more than seven?'

'Yes, Pooh,' said Kanga patiently. 'You're ninety years old, which calls for a celebration.'

'A celebration?' said Eeyore, gloomily. 'A song and dance? I suppose I am ninety, too. That explains a great deal. But no whooping and whatnot for Eeyore.'

'Ninety-two?' asked Piglet, a little confused. 'But if Pooh is only ninety ...'

At which point Tigger bounced up and Piglet sat down in a hurry.

You see, someone had heard, and another person had mentioned, and then somebody had decided that it was time to share some more of Winnie-the-Pooh's adventures. As being ninety years old was a Very Great Thing.

So all the animals in the Forest came together to hear the stories for themselves. Pooh had, in all the excitement, forgotten what many of them are about and hoped that his friends were in them and that he came off All Right.

Well, Pooh needn't have worried. In these adventures he encounters mythical creatures, mysterious new friends (and foes), and a peculiar type of sauce … They're the kind of adventures that just seem to happen in the Hundred Acre Wood.

So settle down, sit back and enjoy four new stories about the Best Bear in All the World, Winnie-the-Pooh, and all his friends.

ACKNOWLEDGMENTS

This official sequel is based on the original Winnie-the-Pooh stories written by A.A.Milne and decorated in the style of E.H.Shepard. The publisher would like to thank the Trustees of the Pooh Properties and The Shepard Trust for their contributions throughout, and Stephanie Thwaites at Curtis Brown for her advice and enthusiasm at all stages of the project.

CONTENTS

AUTUMN 1
in which Pooh and Piglet prepare
to meet a Dragon
PAUL BRIGHT

WINTER 29
in which Penguin arrives in the Forest
BRIAN SIBLEY

SPRING 57
in which Eeyore suspects Another Donkey
is after his thistles
JEANNE WILLIS

SUMMER 81
in which Pooh dreams of the Sauce of the Nile
KATE SAUNDERS

AFTERWORD   105

Autumn

*in which Pooh and Piglet prepare
to meet a Dragon*

BY
PAUL BRIGHT

CHRISTOPHER ROBIN WAS NOT TO BE DISTURBED. 'I'm going to be St George in the village play,' he explained to Pooh, as they kicked through the autumn leaves. 'I have to fight a fire-breathing dragon who has been eating damsels.' He showed Pooh his St George wooden sword. 'And I've got a helmet somewhere ... but, you see, the thing is, I've got lots to say, so I have to learn my words. That's what actors do, and they must not be disturbed.'

Pooh thought about this, then asked:

'This dragon. Does it ... does it live anywhere near the Hundred Acre Wood? Because, if it does, you might let it know that this is not the best place for finding dams ... dams ... what you said.' Then Pooh had another thought, even more alarming. 'And can you tell it that there's no spare honey around here, either. Not even five fresh pots, sitting in anyone's cupboard.'

'Oh, Bear,' said Christopher Robin. 'Dragons are mythical creatures. Or are they extinct? It's one or the other, so there's nothing to worry about. And they don't eat honey. Now, I must go. Please tell everybody – Do Not Disturb!' Then Christopher Robin ran back to the house, making dragon-threatening thrusts and slashes at the undergrowth, while Pooh wondered whether he preferred his dragons mithickle or ex-stinkt and quite what the difference might be.

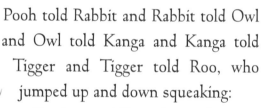

Pooh told Rabbit and Rabbit told Owl and Owl told Kanga and Kanga told Tigger and Tigger told Roo, who jumped up and down squeaking:

'Look at me! I'm a dragon!'

Then Tigger told everyone he bumped into, including Piglet and Eeyore, so that very soon all the Forest knew about St George and the fire-breathing dragon, and that Christopher Robin was Not To Be Disturbed.

* * *

Eeyore did not normally venture far from his gloomy place, but now that summer was over it was gloomier

than ever, and friends were not
dropping by like they used to.

'Not that Like They Used
To was ever what you'd call
Often,' muttered Eeyore. Of
course, Christopher Robin used
to pass by every now and then.

'Well, more Then, than Now,' thought Eeyore, because
now Christopher Robin was Not To Be Disturbed. 'And
no one has Not Disturbed him more than me, these
last few days.' Then Eeyore had an idea. 'I shall go for a
walk,' he announced to himself. 'A stroll. A ramble. And
maybe I shall meet somebody. Or maybe, when I return,
somebody will have dropped by. Or maybe ...' – he let
out a sigh – '... not.'

But Eeyore had walked no more than a dozen plods,
when he saw it. A Something. A Something half hidden
under a bush. A Something that glinted in an Interesting
sort of way.

'Whatever that is,' thought Eeyore. 'I, Eeyore, have
found it.' But try as he might, with hooves and head
and teeth, he couldn't persuade it to come free. 'What
is needed,' he decided at last, 'is assistance. Assistance in
the digging of it out and then assistance in the knowing
of what it is.' He thought maybe Rabbit could help,

'because Rabbit can burrow, and Rabbit has Brain.' But then Rabbit might take charge and maybe even claim the credit for finding the Something Interesting himself. 'Perhaps Owl?' he thought. But Owl did confuse him with very long words. Eeyore ummed and then he aahed. He went this way and then he went that way. And at last he decided that the only thing to do was

to stand and guard the Something Interesting until somebody came along. So he stood, and guarded, and waited, as the wind blew and the leaves swirled and the sun sank ever lower in the sky.

The next morning, Pooh was also pondering where summer had gone, because it was rather too chilly for a Bear to sit outside and have a little something to start the day. But then again it wasn't yet winter, when a Bear pulls up his eiderdown and has a little something warm

and snug before climbing out of bed. It was a time when the weather didn't quite know what to do with itself, and on this particular morning, neither did Pooh. He kicked at the leaves on the path, and as he kicked, he realised that he was heading towards Piglet's house, which seemed the very best thing to do. A hum started forming in his brain; a hum that fitted in nicely with the rhythm of a bear walking and kicking.

Some days are good for a Piglet (*kick*),
To come and visit a Pooh (*kick*).
And there are days
When contrariways
Is the perfect thing to do (*kick*).

He wasn't sure that 'contrariways' was a proper word, but it fitted and it rhymed, and that was all that any useful word needed to do. Pooh was about to start on a second verse when he found that he had already reached Piglet's house. Pooh was sure it was Piglet's house, but it didn't look quite like Piglet's house, because there was a notice on the door, and there had not been a notice on Piglet's door for as long as Pooh could remember (which was generally since a week last Saturday, more or less). But it must be Piglet's house, because there, standing in the doorway, was …

'Hullo, Piglet,' said Pooh, cheerily.

Piglet jumped so hard he fell and landed flat on his bottom.

'Oh! ... Oh! ... Pooh,' he said, rubbing where it hurt. 'It's you. I thought you might be the dragon.'

Pooh stared at Piglet's notice.

DEER DRAGUN
NO DAMSENS HEER
PIGLIT IS OWT (GON AWAY)

'It's for the dragon,' said Piglet. 'To tell him that I'm not at home.'

'But you are at home,' said Pooh. 'And I've come to visit you.'

'Of course I'm at home when you come to visit,' said Piglet. 'But I'm not at home if a dragon visits. Even if I am, if you see what I mean.' Pooh didn't see at all, but Piglet continued: 'It's because I had a frightening dream. I think it was a dragon dream, though it's difficult to know when you've never seen a dragon.'

'I've never seen a Heffalump,' said Pooh, 'but I still dream about them. But Christopher Robin said dragons are mithickle or ex-stinkt, so ... so there's nothing to worry about.' Pooh didn't quite know why there was

7

nothing to worry about, but Christopher Robin had said it, so it must be true.

'There may be nothing for Christopher Robin to worry about,' said Piglet. 'But what if the dragon visits while Christopher Robin is Not To Be Disturbed?'

Pooh scratched his head. He much preferred questions of the 'What would you like?' or 'How about some more?' variety, but he did his best.

'You could say: "Go away, you're only mithickle",' he suggested. 'Or "Please move on now, you're ex-stinkt".'

'I'm not sure that I could,' said Piglet. 'Oh, if only I were brave. I'm not sure that I'm quite ready to meet a dragon. Besides, we don't know What this dragon looks like, or When it's coming, or Where, or anything!'

'Christopher Robin must know,' said Pooh. 'But if we can't ask Christopher Robin about the dragon, there is only one other person wise enough to talk to!'

So off they walked in the direction of Owl's house. But they had not gone far when Piglet suddenly stopped. He grasped Pooh's paw and squeaked:

'We're too late! Look! Under that pile of leaves! It's the dragon!'

Pooh looked. The pile of leaves was rustling … and rising … and groaning …

'GRRRRRR! … OOOOOOH! … AAAAAAH!'

'I can see its nose!' wailed Piglet. 'It's snarling! It's snorting!' He turned to run away, but tripped and fell with a Bump, then lay on the ground covering his eyes with his ears.

The dragon's terrible mouth appeared, grim and grey … and strangely familiar.

'Hullo, Pooh,' said the dragon.

'It's Eeyore!' said Pooh.

Eeyore gave himself a good shake. 'And Piglet too! About time. I was hoping for someone of Considerable Brain, but there it is. You can't have everything.'

Eeyore brushed a leaf from between his ears and

explained that he was guarding a Something Interesting and that he must have been there all night, and what with the wind and the leaves ... 'And now here you are.'

'What was that you said,' asked Pooh hopefully, 'about a Something?'

'It's here,' said Eeyore proudly, showing them the Something Interesting, still firmly stuck under the bush. 'Where I found it. Rabbit could dig it out, of course,' continued Eeyore. 'And Owl could maybe say just what it is. But they're not here. And I could go and find them, but somebody has to guard it. In case ...' He tailed off, not quite sure what the Something Interesting might do in his absence, but wanting to stay anyway, to be sure.

'Why don't I go and fetch Rabbit,' said Pooh, quite forgetting for the moment about the dragon.

'And I'll go and talk to Owl,' said Piglet, who had not forgotten at all.

'That would be most satisfactory,' said Eeyore, solemnly continuing with his guard duties.

Piglet hurried to Owl's house as fast as his little legs would take him. He pulled gently at the bell-pull because it seemed the polite thing to do, then he knocked loudly at the knocker, because everybody knew that Owl's bell-rope, though it looked very grand, was not in fact attached to a bell.

'Piglet!' exclaimed Owl. 'What a pleasure to see you.'

Piglet explained about Eeyore and the Something Interesting, and the need for someone who knew something about Somethings to come and look at it. Owl did his best to look wise, and told Piglet that

nobody knew anything about Anything as much as he, Owl, knew something about Somethings. He was heading towards the front door when Piglet said:

'Then there's the dragon ...' He explained in a great rush about not knowing the What and the Where and the When of the fire-breathing dragon, or even whether it was mithickle or ex-stinkt. And how he and Pooh, Pooh and he, thought that someone as wise as Owl could maybe explain.

'Indeed!' said Owl, thinking quickly. 'Now, let me see. Well ... something is ex-stinkt if ... if it was previously, so far as anyone can recall, stinkt, but is not, as far as anyone can substantiate, stinkt any more.' He glanced at Piglet who looked suitably impressed, so Owl continued. 'As for mithickle creatures, well ... they are creatures that are sadly mithed – most people wish they were still around even though they have not been seen for as long as anyone can remember. Now is that clear?'

'Oh yes, yes. Thank you,' said Piglet, and Owl turned to leave when Piglet continued, 'So, if a mithickle creature hasn't been seen for as long as anyone can remember, which Pooh says is a week last Saturday, when might it come back again?'

Owl was rather taken aback by this.

'Umm,' he said. Then 'Aah.' Then 'Umm,' once again. And at last: 'Well, more or less, plus or minus, give or take, and of course allowing for the usual errors and omissions, one wouldn't expect to see a dragon again until at least a week next Tuesday.'

Owl hurried outside before Piglet could come up

with any more difficult questions. Then he flew from branch to branch while Piglet scurried back along the forest path. Owl started telling Piglet the hilarious tale of his Great Aunt Agatha's embarrassing experience in Timbuktu, but Piglet didn't seem to be listening. And just then:

'Aah! Here's Eeyore,' said Owl. 'And if I'm not mistaken, here come Pooh and Rabbit.'

Rabbit quickly got to work. There were sounds of digging and delving, then he reappeared proudly holding

the Something Interesting. He rubbed off some lumps and streaks of mud and it glinted in a way that only Something Interesting can.

'Pooh!' whispered Piglet, urgently, but Rabbit said: '*Sshhh!*' very firmly and started to examine the Something, turning it in his paws.

'Hmmm!' he said. 'Obviously some sort of container. For putting things in.'

'Like honey?' suggested Pooh.

'Or haycorns,' said Piglet, who really thought the arrival of a dragon a week next Tuesday much more important, but didn't want to be '*Sshhh'd*' at again.

'Quite,' said Rabbit, briskly. 'So what we have found is …'

'What *I* have found,' interrupted Eeyore, who had been expecting this. 'Eeyore. Found. It.'

'Yes, yes,' said Rabbit, 'what Eeyore has found …'

'Don't mention it,' said Eeyore.

'… is, as I said, some sort of container. The question is, how old is it? Is it, for example, BC or AD?'

Pooh stared at the sky, thinking it was a bit late in the year for bee seeing.

'In my own opinion,' continued Rabbit, 'I would suggest it is BC because it Badly needs Cleaning.'

'Quite so,' interrupted Owl, peering intently at the Something. 'But then again it may well be AD since it is Antique and Dirty, or even 'Ardly Damaged. Personally,' he added, 'I would say it has something of the Etruscan period about it.' Owl couldn't remember where he had heard the word Etruscan, but it was one of those words you don't often get the chance to use, and he wanted to make the most of this opportunity.

'Pooh!' whispered Piglet again, but now Owl looked at him in a most severe manner.

'It is quite possibly of such antiquity,' said Rabbit. He glanced at Owl in case the Etruscans were not of much antiquity at all, but had been roaming the Forest filling their containers with haycorns and honey just yesterday, but Owl did not argue. 'In addition,' said Rabbit ...

But Piglet could contain himself no longer.

'A dragon's coming!' he squeaked, at the top of his voice. 'A fire-breathing dragon – a week next Tuesday. What are we going to do?'

Piglet explained what Owl had said, and how the dragon was probably on its way already, with nostrils glowing, intent on arriving in the Forest in just a few days.

'More or less,' added Owl, who was beginning to wonder if he had been totally accurate in his prediction. 'Give or take.'

'If only Christopher Robin were here,' squeaked Piglet. 'Maybe we should disturb him, just for a moment.'

'He was very insis … instis … he did tell me twice,' said Pooh.

'Then we have to be prepared,' said Rabbit. 'We must have a Plan. Someone else must be ready to fight the dragon.'

There was a short pause, followed by a longer one, and interrupted by much shuffling of feet and clearing of throats. A third pause arrived and took over where the previous one had left off.

Piglet shut his eyes and closed his mouth tightly, just in case he squeaked or sneezed and somebody thought he was saying: 'Me!' But all of a sudden he did say something.

'Ow!' he burst out, then found himself face down on the ground again. Something very large was sitting on him. Piglet waited for a blast of fiery breath and hoped that his ears wouldn't get too singed. But what he heard was Roo's tiny voice saying:

'Look everybody! Tigger's playing "Squeak, Piglet. Squeak"!'

And Kanga's not so tiny voice saying, severely:

'Tigger, you must learn not to bounce so. Now let Piglet go.'

And, striding along the path behind them, came Christopher Robin.

Piglet picked himself up. The world was suddenly a wonderful place. Above him the sun was shining, and he felt the joy one can only know when a fierce dragon, or even just a bouncy Tigger, has been lifted off of one's shoulders.

'Hullo, Pooh!' said Christopher Robin. 'And Piglet and Eeyore and Owl and Rabbit. I've finished learning my words now. I'm all ready to be St George.'

There was a short silence, and more shuffling of feet.

'About St George,' began Pooh. 'Well ... the thing is ... Owl thinks ...'

'... And Rabbit thinks ...' said Owl, quickly.

'... And Piglet thinks ...' said Rabbit.

'... We all think ...' said Piglet.

'Don't bring me into this,' said Eeyore. 'Nobody asked my opinion.'

'... Anyway,' continued Pooh, 'there is a fire-breathing dragon coming to the wood a week next Tuesday, possibly in search of damsons. And we hoped, maybe, you might be able to persuade it ... not to stay too long.'

Christopher Robin tried not to laugh.
He looked around at his friends.
Rabbit was still holding the
Something Interesting.

'My helmet!' cried
Christopher Robin. 'You've
found my St George helmet!'
He put the Etruscan container on
his head. 'I put it down just here a few days ago, then couldn't find it again. Oh, well done!'

'A helmet?' said Rabbit. 'Yes! Of course. We've found your helmet.'

There was a loud cough close to Rabbit's ear.

'I mean ... Eeyore found your helmet.'

'All on his own,' said Eeyore. 'But don't mention it.'

Christopher Robin hugged Eeyore's neck.

'You are the very best of donkeys,' he said.

Eeyore looked down at his hooves in an embarrassed sort of way, and his nose turned a slightly pinker shade of grey.

'And about dragons,' continued Christopher Robin. 'Well, they're only in stories ... and plays of course.

And I happen to know, I just do, that there aren't any real live dragons in this story.'

'There you are,' said Pooh to Piglet, 'didn't I say all along there was nothing to worry about?'

* * *

Owl and Rabbit had gone. Kanga had taken Roo and Tigger home for their dose of Strengthening Medicine, and Eeyore had wandered back to his Lonely Place, muttering softly: 'Best of donkeys. Me. Eeyore!'

Christopher Robin and Pooh and Piglet walked here and there but nowhere in particular, and Christopher Robin explained that mythical was rather like pretend, and that extinct meant creatures that weren't here any more, and that the dragon he was fighting in the play

wasn't real either, but made of bits of wood and fabric stuck together.

'If there were a real fire-breathing dragon,' he said, 'which there isn't, but just if there were, then even the very bravest person, or bear, or Piglet, would be frightened. They would just pretend not to be, because that's what being brave is all about.'

Pooh asked who the very bravest person, or bear, or Piglet was. Christopher Robin ummed and aahed just a little, and then said that, although he couldn't say for the whole wide world, he was probably the bravest person in the Forest, and Pooh was the bravest bear, and Piglet was definitely the bravest Piglet. Pooh felt quite happy to be the Bravest Bear now there was no dragon to fight, but Piglet couldn't help wondering how he could be the bravest Piglet in the Forest when he was also the only Piglet in the Forest. He was just going to ask about this, when Christopher Robin, who always seemed to know what everyone was thinking, said:

'I quite fancy a Little Something. How about you?'

And, of course, they did.

WINTER

in which Penguin arrives in the Forest

BY

BRIAN SIBLEY

ONE MORNING, WINNIE-THE-POOH LOOKED OUT of his window and saw something that took him by surprise. 'This is very Strange and Unusual,' said Pooh, 'but, unless I'm mistaken, somebody has taken the Forest away and put a lot of Something White there instead.'

This was confusing and, since it was still rather early and he hadn't yet had his first pot of honey, Pooh thought a moment and said, 'No, that can't be it, because it would be really most unlikely,' and then added, 'so what must have happened is that somebody has taken my house and put it somewhere else altogether, where it is very white.'

And then, as there were still bits of Pooh's brain that were feeling sleepy, he decided that he'd better take another look.

'Ah, *now* I understand,' said Pooh, slowly. 'It's been

snowing. Yes, that's it,' he went on, 'like that time when Piglet and I nearly caught a Woozle – or was it a Wizzle that nearly caught us? Well, anyway, that explains everything.'

Mentioning Piglet made Pooh think of something else.

'The trouble with snow,' he said, 'is that, unless you are very careful, you can Get Snowed-In which, if you are a very small animal like Piglet, can be Bothersome and Alarming. So maybe I ought to go and see if Piglet has Got Snowed-In and needs help with Getting Snowed-Out.'

So, off he stumped to the nearest cupboard where he was sure of finding a pot or two of something, and had one jar of honey, and then another one to warm himself because he had just remembered that snow had an unpleasant habit of being cold on the toes. Then, noticing that it was now snowing again, very hard, he decided to have another small jar, 'Just in case,' he said.

When he had licked the very last lick, Winnie-the-Pooh put on his scarf and opened his front door into a Hundred Acre Wood that was very white and still.

Heading in what he thought was the general direction of Piglet's house (it was difficult to be certain with so much snow about), Pooh remembered having once thought up a hum such as could be happily hummed in snowy weather, and decided he would think up a new one. It went:

It can snow just a little
Or it can snow quite a lot,
But it hardly ever snows
When the weather is hot.

Pooh was very pleased that a rhyme had come along just in time to meet the last line as it arrived, and went on ...

And it's also said
(And I think it's right)
That it seldom ever snows
When the sun is bright.

Just then something happened that made him forget his hum completely. Someone was coming towards him through the snow with a curious waddling way of walking. It was a strange-looking creature that seemed to be mostly black and white with a hint of yellow about the feet and what was a rather beaky face.

'Hullo,' said Pooh.

The Someone stopped waddling and stood very still in front of Pooh. He opened what was definitely a beak and then snapped it shut again without saying anything.

'I said "Hullo",' said Pooh.

This time, the Someone turned its head to one side, closed its eyes and shifted awkwardly to and fro on its yellow feet, but said nothing.

Thinking that perhaps it might be hard of hearing, Pooh spoke again, only this time slowly and very loudly.

'I SAID, "I SAID, 'HULLO' ",'.

'I heard you the first time,' the Someone muttered in a low, embarrassed voice, still not looking at Pooh, 'and, if you'll forgive me mentioning it, I heard you the second and third times as well!'

'Oh, why didn't you answer me?' asked Pooh.

'Because,' it replied apologetically, 'we have not been properly introduced.'

'Well, I'm Winnie-the-Pooh,' said Bear, 'or Pooh for short. Who are you?'

'Oh, dear, oh, dear,' muttered the Someone, anxiously, looking as if he would rather have been somewhere else. 'The thing is, you see,' he said, giving a nervous flap of what looked like a small pair of wings, 'you can only be introduced to Someone by Someone Else.'

Pooh didn't know what to say to this, so instead he arranged his scarf, hoping to stop more snow from going down the back of his neck in that uncomfortable, tickly way.

'You see,' the creature went on, 'it's a matter of etiquette.'

Pooh was about to ask, 'Eti-what?', wondering whether it might have anything to do with food, when Rabbit came hurrying through a snowdrift that had once been a forest path, looking very flustered.

'Hullo, Rabbit,' said Pooh.

'Do you happen to have a spade I can borrow?' replied Rabbit who, having a front door and a back door, had Got Snowed-In twice over, as it were.

Pooh said that the last time he'd needed one he'd borrowed Christopher Robin's and so Rabbit said he'd go and ask him instead.

'Rabbit,' said Pooh, 'may I ask you something?'

'Can't it wait until I've shifted the snow out of my second-best bedroom?'

'Not really,' said Pooh. And then, holding up his paw so he could whisper behind it, he asked Rabbit if he knew anything about the Black-and-White Whatever-it-was that was standing nearby in the snow.

'Of course,' said Rabbit. 'He's new. Christopher Robin said he was coming.' Lowering his voice, he added: 'He's very shy and very proper. Christopher Robin said he needs Bringing Out of Himself. And now,' said Rabbit, in his normal voice again, 'I really have to be going, because when you've got snow under your bed, you just have to do something about it.'

'Yes, of course,' said Pooh, adding in a whisper again, 'but would you mind introducing us before you go?'

Rabbit tutted impatiently. 'Pooh, meet Penguin,' he said. 'Penguin, meet Pooh.' And with that he vanished in a whirl of snowflakes ...

'Hullo, Penguin!' said Pooh.

'Hullo, Pooh!' said Penguin. 'It's very nice to meet you.'

And, having got over the difficult business of introductions, Penguin seemed a little more at ease, and stopped hopping awkwardly from one foot to another. Wondering if it might help Bring Penguin Out of Himself, Pooh asked whether, if he weren't in a hurry to do anything else, he might like to come along with him to visit Piglet. Penguin politely replied that, yes, thank you, if that wasn't too much trouble, he should like that very much indeed.

So off they went, Pooh stumping along with Penguin waddling by his side.

'Where did you come from?' asked Pooh.

'Oh, you know,' replied Penguin vaguely.

'Ah,' said Pooh, who didn't.

'The Usual Place actually,' added Penguin.

There was an awkward silence for a few minutes while Pooh tried to remember where that was and, when he couldn't, he said: 'Oh, well, I expect Christopher Robin knows.'

'Oh, yes,' said Penguin, 'Christopher Robin knows everything. He said that, most of the time, Generally Speaking, Penguins are found at the South Pole.'

'Well, well,' said Pooh, very much surprised. 'A South Pole? I didn't know there was another one at the other end.' And then, because Penguin looked puzzled, he explained, '*I* discovered the North Pole, you know.'

'Really?' said Penguin, sounding impressed. 'I should rather like to discover something someday. But I expect it takes a lot of Brain.'

Pooh was about to explain that he had really only discovered the North Pole by accident, and that actually he was a Bear of No Brain at all, when he saw Piglet battling his way through the blizzard towards them.

Now, the Piglet was on his way to see Pooh to ask whether he thought it was going to Go On Snowing for Very Long. His little head was down and the snow was getting in his eyes and his ears and making it difficult to see and hear anything. So, when Pooh suddenly said, 'Hullo, Piglet, this is Penguin,' he jumped with surprise.

Piglet jumped again when he saw Penguin for the first time and noticed how very beaky he was, but not wanting the strange creature to think him of a Nervous Disposition, he decided to jump up and down in a Keeping Warm sort of way.

'This is Piglet, Penguin.'

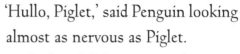

'Hullo, Piglet,' said Penguin looking almost as nervous as Piglet.

Piglet didn't answer, but just kept looking at Penguin's beak.

'You have to say, "Hullo," back,' whispered Pooh. 'It's all to do with something that sounds as if it were to do with eating, but probably isn't.'

Piglet said 'Oh,' and then, 'Hullo, Penguin.' And Penguin said, 'Very nice to meet you,' and Piglet said, 'Likewise, I'm sure.' And then, in a whisper, asked Pooh, 'I was wondering about the beak. Is he *safe*?'

'I think so,' Pooh whispered back, adding, 'Christopher Robin knows all about him, but says he needs Bringing Out of Himself. He's from the Usual Place, you know.'

'Ah,' said Piglet, who didn't, and in order to keep from thinking about Penguin's beak, he asked him whether he had met Owl, who also had a beak, even though it wasn't anywhere near as beaky as this one.

'I'm afraid not,' said Penguin apologetically.

'In that case,' said Pooh, who had been trying to think

of ways to Bring a Penguin Out of Himself, 'I shall introduce you.'

So Pooh led the way through the Hundred Acre Wood, stopping every now and then to help Piglet, who only had short legs and, as the snow was falling heavily, kept finding himself up to his nose and, sometimes, his ears. Penguin, on the other hand, waddled happily along without any difficulty at all.

When they reached The Chestnuts, Pooh climbed up to Owl's front door and knocked. And knocked. And *knocked*. It took a great deal of knocking to get an answer from Owl, who was sitting by the fire studying the newspaper, which he did with it spread out over his closed eyes while making a thoughtful snoring sound.

'Hullo, Owl,' said Pooh, when Owl finally opened the door, 'there's a new bird come to live in the Forest and we've brought him to see you because he needs Bringing

Out of Himself.'

'Aha!' replied Owl. 'Well, as they say, birds of a feather flock together! Where is he?'

'Down there, with Piglet,' said Pooh, adding helpfully, 'the taller black-and-white one on the left.'

Owl put on his glasses, peered over the top of them, then took them off quickly, saying in a low voice: 'Sorry, Pooh, can't help. Most regrettable, but quite impossible.'

'But,' said, Pooh, 'I thought you said, "Birds of a feather ..."'

'Yes,' said Owl, 'usually, but I didn't know your friend was a ...' he hesitated and then started spelling out the word.

'P – E – N ...' he began and then stopped, trying to remember exactly what came next, before realising that it didn't matter because Pooh couldn't spell anyway.

Covering his confusion with a cough, Owl went on: 'The trouble is, Pooh, your friend down there has tiny little wings that are, unfortunately, Aerodynamically Inadequate.'

Pooh was about to ask what that meant when Owl added, 'Or, to put it simply, some birds can fly and some can't, and that's all there is to it!'

It was at this precise second that an agitated Rabbit suddenly came scurrying along, talking so excitedly that he was fast running out of breath.

'He wasn't in … Went to borrow his spade … For the snow, you see … But he's not there … Gone!'

'Who's gone?' asked Pooh, climbing down from Owl's front door.

'Christopher Robin, of course,' said Rabbit.

'Gone where?' asked Piglet anxiously.

'And why?' added Owl, flying down to join the others.

'That,' said Rabbit, 'is what I have been asking myself ever since I found the note.'

'Note?' asked Pooh, Piglet and Owl all at once.

'Pinned on his door,' explained Rabbit, producing a piece of paper with large letters written on it.

'This requires looking into,' said Owl pompously, and taking the

paper he examined it this way and that, finally deciding that the best way of reading it was upside down.

'What does it say?' asked Pooh.

'Well ...' said Owl.

'The thing is ...' said Owl.

'What it says ...' said Owl, 'is most interesting and, of course, explains everything!'

'It does?' asked Pooh.

'Oh, yes! What it says is –'

'What it says,' said Rabbit crossly, taking back the piece of paper and turning it the right way up, 'is "GON TO BOGANIN. C.R."'

'Gone where?' asked Piglet, who didn't like to think of Christopher Robin being anywhere else.

'GON TO BOGANIN,' repeated Rabbit.

'No such place!' snorted Owl.

'Well,' said Rabbit, 'that's what it says.'

'Nonsense!' Owl went on. 'I know every inch of the Hundred Acre Wood and I've never heard of it.'

'In that case,' said Pooh, 'we must find out where this whatever-it's-called place is and look for Christopher Robin.'

'Exactly!' said Rabbit, taking charge. 'We will organise a search, immediately. And we must question everyone. It is essential that we establish who was the last person to see Christopher Robin.'

'Excuse me,' said a soft voice behind them, 'but I was.'

It was Penguin. Everyone had quite forgotten about him, but now they all turned and stared at him open-mouthed.

'You?' asked Owl at last, sounding a little annoyed.

'Yes,' said Penguin, feeling rather awkward at being looked at by everyone. 'I was with him just a little while ago.' Then, after a pause, he added, 'I can take you to him, if you like.'

'In that case,' said Owl, fluffing up his feathers in a huffy sort of way, 'if you'll excuse me, I'll get back to my newspaper.' And with that he flew up to his front door,

and went inside, closing it with a bang.

The others were still staring at Penguin who looked at the sky and then at his feet before saying shyly,

'Shall we go?'

So they went.

It had stopped snowing when they arrived. It was still cold, but the grey clouds had blown away, leaving a clear blue sky and the snow sparkling in the sun. They were at the very top of the Forest and there was Christopher Robin in his big boots, wrapped up warm and waving to them. Everybody suddenly felt very cheerful, even Rabbit who was still worried about the amount of snow that, by now, was probably piling up against his wardrobe doors.

'Hullo, everyone,' said Christopher Robin, 'you've met Penguin, I see.'

They all said 'Hullo', and yes they had and Pooh explained that they'd thought he had gone off to somewhere called 'Boganin', and then Christopher Robin started to laugh.

'I said, I'd gone tobogganing!' he explained and pointed to something made of wood that was flat with a turned-up end and was gleaming with shiny, new, red paint against the snow.

'It's a toboggan for sliding downhill on the snow. Watch!'

Christopher Robin jumped on the toboggan and went dashing off down the hillside very fast. When he reached the bottom, he got off and began climbing up again, pulling the toboggan behind him.

'Now,' said Christopher Robin when he got back to the top. 'Who wants to go next?'

Everyone looked a little doubtful, but then seeing as Christopher Robin was enjoying it so much, thought why shouldn't they try it too. Rabbit went first; then Pooh and Piglet went together, with Piglet holding tightly and keeping his eyes firmly shut.

When it came to Penguin's turn, he hung back, saying in a very small voice, 'I'm not sure if I can.'

'Come on, Penguin!' said Christopher Robin encouragingly.

Penguin still looked uncertain, but after taking a deep breath, he waddled towards the toboggan and sat down on it gingerly. And, after a gentle push from Christopher Robin, he took off with a whoosh.

At first Penguin was doing rather well and was picking up speed nicely. 'He's quite good, isn't he,' Pooh said to

49

Piglet, but suddenly the toboggan collided with a big stone sticking up out of the snow. It gave a sudden lurch and threw Penguin right off.

Everyone held their breath and Christopher Robin was about to call out to see if Penguin was all right when he realised that he didn't need to. The toboggan had stopped, but Penguin had kept on going. Lying flat on his tummy, and propelling himself along with his little wings, he was now flying gracefully along over the snow.

When he arrived at the bottom of the hill, the spectators cheered, and Pooh said something Very Wise Indeed: 'Some birds can toboggan, and others can't, and that's all there is to it!'

And that was that. Penguin was so delighted to find that he could go tobogganing without a toboggan, that he went up and down, and up and down, and then up and down again.

Then they all spent the next hour happily having races: Pooh and Rabbit taking turns to ride with Christopher Robin while

Piglet rode on Penguin's back, alternately laughing and squeaking excitedly, then keeping his eyes firmly shut.

'I really must be getting back,' Rabbit said eventually. 'My house won't un-snow itself you know.'

He picked up Christopher Robin's spade, which he'd brought with him, in case of mishaps while tobogganing, and hurried off to start digging.

Penguin was asking Christopher Robin if they had time for just one more race when Pooh whispered to Piglet that he thought they had finally managed to Bring Penguin Out of Himself and Piglet whispered back that he thought so too.

That was when Pooh had an Idea. 'Here is Penguin,' he said, 'a visitor to the Hundred Acre Wood and yet none of us have invited him to come and visit. So, since it must be nearly time for a smackerel of something, let's go home and have some honey –'

'And haycorns,' added Piglet.

'And haycorns,' said Pooh, 'and mugs of hot chocolate.'

'Pardon me,' said Penguin, 'please don't think me rude, but you see, I'm not really an indoors kind of bird. I much prefer being out in the snow.'

Pooh thought for a moment and then he had Another Idea. 'Well,' he said, 'that being so, why don't we have a Special Winter Picnic? I always think things taste better out of doors.'

Christopher Robin gave Pooh an admiring look as if to say, 'Clever Old Bear!' and turned to see what Penguin thought.

'That sounds perfect,' said Penguin happily and it was settled.

So, Pooh hurried home to get a jar of honey, and another scarf, while Piglet scampered off to get some of his best haycorns.

And when they got back to the forest, Christopher

Robin produced three mugs of steaming hot chocolate and an ice lollipop for Penguin and the Special Winter Picnic was a great success.

* * *

It was a day or two later when the snow had, at last, started to thaw, that Pooh went to see how Penguin was getting along, but there was no sign of him anywhere. Pooh was puzzling about this when Christopher Robin came along.

'Hullo, Bear,' he said.

'Hullo,' replied Pooh, 'where's Penguin?'

'He's gone,' said Christopher Robin, carelessly.

'Oh,' said Pooh in surprise.

'On account of the snow,' explained Christopher Robin.

Pooh looked confused. 'But the snow's almost melted.'

'That was the trouble,' said Christopher Robin. 'It was getting too warm for him.'

'So where did he go?' asked Pooh.

'Oh, you know,' Christopher Robin replied vaguely.

'Ah, yes,' said Pooh, who still didn't.

'Well, then,' said Christopher Robin.

'Well, then,' said Pooh.

And there not being a lot more to say, they set off for home.

'Will Penguin come back?' asked Pooh.

'Maybe,' said Christopher Robin.

'Perhaps he'll come and visit next winter,' said Pooh.

'He might,' said Christopher Robin.

They walked on in silence for a while and Pooh was thoughtful. 'I've been thinking, Christopher Robin,' said Pooh, 'which do you like best: old friends or new?'

Christopher Robin thought and, after a long time, said: 'Well, I like new friends because you never quite know what they'll do next. But I like old friends, too, because, however long you've known them, you are always discovering things that you didn't know before.'

Spring

in which Eeyore suspects Another Donkey is after his thistles

BY

JEANNE WILLIS

SPRING WAS IN THE AIR. THE SUN WAS SHINING, the birds were nesting and Winnie-the-Pooh was stumping along by the boggy end of the Forest admiring the daffodils and humming to himself when he bumped into his old friend, Eeyore.

'Tra la la and a tiddle-tiddle-pom,' hummed Pooh, 'Good morning, Eeyore!'

'Tra la la?' said Eeyore, glumly. 'Good morning? Not for me, it isn't. I was as happy as a lark earlier. I might have known it wouldn't last.'

Pooh gazed up at the clear blue sky.

'It's a beautiful day,' he said.

'Not from where I'm sitting,' replied Eeyore.

'Try standing next to me,' said Pooh. 'With a tiddle-tiddle-pom.'

Eeyore stood next to Pooh, but after a while, he shook his head.

'It's not working.' He sighed. 'It's all right for you, full of the Joys of Spring, but what have I got to sing about, Pooh?'

Pooh scratched his head and thought. It was a bit early for thinking but just then he noticed a fresh patch of thistles growing by the pond. They were exactly the sort that Eeyore liked most, so Pooh said:

'Eeyore, you could sing a song of thistles.'

'Why would I?' said Eeyore.

'Because it's a Munching kind of song and thistles make you happy,' said Pooh.

Eeyore hung his head.

'They did once,' he groaned. 'Earlier, when I saw those new thistles I said, "Hurrah, the more the merrier!" If I'd known he had his eye on them, I'd never have got my hopes up.'

'He who?' asked Pooh.

'Hee Haw!' said Eeyore, 'There's Another Donkey. I suspect he's after my thistles and he didn't look like the sort of donkey who likes sharing.'

Pooh could hardly believe his ears.

'There's Another Donkey?' he said. 'In this Forest?'

'The very same,' replied Eeyore. 'And I don't like the look of him one bit.'

'What did he look like?' wondered Pooh.

'This!' said Eeyore, pulling the sort of face a donkey makes when it's about to eat another donkey's thistles. Pooh was so startled, he sat down with a bump.

'I don't like the look of him either!' he said. 'Where is he now?'

Eeyore gave a sad little shrug.

'That's a good question, Pooh. I was hoping you might know the answer.'

'So was I,' said Pooh.

'I would go and look for him,' said Eeyore. 'But if I go, he will come and eat all my thistles without so much as a please or thank you.'

'Will he?' said Pooh.

'Of course. He's Another Donkey. It's what donkeys do,' said Eeyore. 'Once he's got a taste for them, he won't leave me so much as a prickle. I shall waste away to a piece of string. Goodbye, Pooh. It was nice knowing you.'

Pooh was a Bear of Very Little Brain, but he knew a Friend In Need when he saw one.

'Eeyore,' he announced, 'I, Winnie-the-Pooh, will do something about this.'

'What sort of something?' asked Eeyore.

Pooh ummed and he aahed and he marched up and down, then he said triumphantly, 'A very BIG something.'

'Good luck,' said Eeyore. 'Meanwhile here am I, fading away ...'

'I shan't be long,' said Pooh.

'How long?' grumbled Eeyore. 'Teatime? Tomorrow? Some time never?'

'Just a bit longer than it takes to fetch Piglet,' said Pooh. 'I would go on my own but finding Another Donkey is always quicker with two.'

With that, he hurried off to Piglet's house, very much hoping that he wouldn't meet Another Donkey on the way.

Piglet was busy doing nothing, but when Pooh arrived and wondered casually if he would help him track down Another Donkey who was after Eeyore's thistles and causing him Great Distress, Piglet said he would be only too pleased, just as long as it didn't look like a Heffalump.

'It doesn't,' said Pooh.

'Did Eeyore say it was fierce?' asked Piglet.

'Not in so many words,' said Pooh. 'It was what he did that bothered me.'

'What did he do, Pooh?' asked Piglet.

'This!' said Pooh, pulling the face of Another Donkey who didn't like sharing. Piglet gave a squeak of fright and fell down quite suddenly. Just then, Rabbit came along, and seeing Piglet lying in the grass, he asked what he was up to.

'I'm busy,' said Piglet.

'Busy doing what?' asked Rabbit.

'Busy doing what Very Small Animals do when asked to track down Very Large Animals they don't like the look of,' whispered Piglet.

Rabbit glanced around cautiously.

'What does this Very Large Animal look like exactly?'

'Show him, Pooh!' said Piglet, squeezing his eyes shut.

Pooh pulled the face he

had pulled before and Rabbit jumped backwards in surprise.

'That looks a bit like Eeyore, only smiling!' he remarked.

'That's because it's Another Donkey,' said Pooh.

'And it's after Eeyore's thistles!' added Piglet. 'Have you stopped pulling that face yet, Pooh?'

Pooh said he had, so Piglet opened his eyes and danced about in an anxious way, squealing, 'Eeyore is in Great Distress! Help! Do something, Rabbit!'

'Me?' said Rabbit. 'Like what, Piglet?'

'Like what, Pooh?' said Piglet.

'Like what, Rabbit?' said Pooh.

Rabbit didn't know, but the longer they wondered what to do, the less thistles there would be for Eeyore so Rabbit counted everyone and noting that Piglet was half the size of Pooh he said, 'There are two and a half of us and only one of him, so if we go together and ask him politely to share, there shouldn't be a problem.'

'What if there isn't only one of him?' said Piglet. 'What if there's another Another Donkey?'

'Piglet has a point …' said Pooh, thoughtfully.

Rabbit added everything up and came to a decision.

'To be on the safe side, I will ask all my friends and relations to come too, along with Kanga and Tigger and –'

'Tigger?' said Piglet doubtfully.

Piglet was very fond of Tigger but he was worried that his bounciness might upset Another Donkey who might not like being bounced and might fly into a rage.

'Yes, Tigger,' said Rabbit firmly. 'The Other Donkey might be one of the fiercer animals, in which case, Tigger will keep him in his place.'

'Not if he bounces him,' said Pooh who had once been bounced by Tigger and ended up in another place entirely.

'That's the beauty of it,' said Rabbit. 'If Tigger comes, he's so bouncy, it will seem like there are more of us than there really are, which is good because there's Safety in Numbers.'

Pooh wasn't good at numbers but the fact that Rabbit had more relatives than he could count was

an Enormous Comfort, so he gave Piglet his paw and gathering Rabbit's friends and relations on the way, they went to find Kanga.

* * *

Kanga was sitting under a pine tree teaching Roo to count.

'Hullo, one Pooh! Hullo, one Piglet! Hullo, one Rabbit!' said Roo. 'Guess what I'm doing? I'm learning to count ... one, two, four, three, five, six!'

'So you are!' said Pooh.

'Talking of numbers, Kanga,' said Rabbit, 'There's

Another Donkey in the wood ...'

'Possibly three!' squeaked Piglet.

'And we were wondering,' continued Rabbit, 'if you would come with us and ask it not to do something. '

'Why, what has it done, dear?' said Kanga.

'It's not what it's done so much as what it might do,' said Pooh. 'It might not share Eeyore's thistles and it's making him gloomy.'

To which Kanga said, 'Tut! We can't have that! Come along, Roo. I think the Other Donkey needs teaching a lesson.'

'Ooh!' said Roo, jumping into Kanga's apron pocket. 'Are you going to teach it to count? I can count ... listen, Piglet! One, three, five, two, four, six!'

'That's the way,' said Piglet, paying more attention to where Tigger wasn't than to Roo's counting. He couldn't see him anywhere, but that didn't mean he wasn't somewhere because Hiding was what Tiggers did best.

'Tigger's gone fishing, dear,' said Kanga.

'When will he be home?' asked Rabbit. 'We were hoping he'd come too.'

'I thought he'd be back by now,' said Kanga. 'But Tigger is big enough to look after himself. I wouldn't worry.'

But Piglet did worry, so Kanga said, 'Come along, Piglet. There will be plenty of us; me, you, Rabbit, Pooh, Roo and ...'

'Roo is too little to count,' said Piglet.

'I *can* count, Piglet!' insisted Roo. 'One, three, two four, five, six!'

Piglet was so impressed with Roo's counting, he said he would come along if he could hide in Kanga's pocket. So, when she'd brushed out the crumbs, he jumped in next to Roo and off they all went to search for the Other Donkey, or three, with Pooh leading the way.

The only problem with Pooh leading the way was that he didn't know where he was going. He did in winter, but now that the bluebells were clumping and the ferns were unfurling, the old, familiar pathways had taken a completely different turn.

'Are we lost?' said Rabbit.

'No,' said Pooh, 'I know *exactly* where we aren't.'

'Is … is it *exactly* the kind of place we might find Another Donkey?' worried Piglet.

'It might be,' said Pooh, but seeing the anxious look on Piglet's face he said, 'Then again, it might not. You never can tell with donkeys.'

Piglet was so glad that it
might not be, he shouted,
'Hooray!' but then, to
his great dismay, he saw
a shadowy Something
that looked suspiciously
like Another Donkey
walking towards them
through the trees.

'Help! It's Him!' squeaked Piglet. 'There he is! Help!'
And Pooh said, 'Well spotted Piglet!' But as it came
closer, he saw how miserable it looked and realised it
wasn't Another Donkey at all.

'It's all right, Piglet. It's only Eeyore,' said Pooh.

'Well, pardon me for being such a disappointment,'
said Eeyore. 'That wasn't quite the warm greeting I was
hoping for. But I've had worse.'

'What are you doing here?' asked Pooh.

'Looking for you,' said Eeyore. 'You said you wouldn't
be long but when you were, I thought something
terrible had happened, like it always does, when all along
you were on a jolly jaunt with your friends, never mind
my thistles!'

'Who is minding your thistles, Eeyore dear?' asked
Kanga. 'It wouldn't do to turn your back on them with

Another Donkey about.'

'Tigger is minding them,' said Eeyore, 'He was about to go fishing in the pond but when I gave him my sad tale ...'

'Your tail does look rather sad,' agreed Pooh. 'Which is what comes of giving it to Tigger.'

Eeyore rolled his eyes.

'I didn't give Tigger my tail. I gave him my sorry *story* and Tigger said if I had to go and find you, he would mind my thistles because that's what Tiggers do best.'

'But what if two more donkeys come along?' said Piglet.

That made Eeyore gloomier than ever, because he knew a thing or two about donkeys and he doubted that even Tigger could bounce three of them.

'I haven't seen Another Donkey since this morning!' he cried. 'Now I know why! He's gone to tell his friends about my thistles. They'll be eating them as we speak.'

'If we hurry and ask them to save you some, I'm sure they'll listen,' said Kanga.

Eeyore shook his head sadly. 'Donkeys never listen.'

Just as all hope of saving Eeyore's thistles seemed to be lost, Pooh had a Good Idea.

'Let's ask Owl what to do,' he said.

Eeyore swivelled one ear and gazed at him mournfully. 'What did you say, Pooh? I wasn't listening.'

So Pooh said it again and as no one had a better idea, off they all went to see Owl.

* * *

Owl was polishing his teapot in readiness for some light refreshment when there was a knock at his door. He was surprised, as he wasn't expecting guests, and had only laid a place for one.

'Who's there?' he called.

'Lots of us,' said Pooh.

Owl opened his door and when he saw how many of them there were, he asked if whatever they wanted could wait until he'd finished his Afternoon Tea.

By now, Pooh was feeling rather rumbly and after hearing the words 'Afternoon Tea', he suggested that Owl invited everybody in to help him finish it.

'I would do,' said Owl. 'But I don't have the requisite amount of crockery.'

'Meaning what?' asked Pooh.

'I haven't got enough plates,' said Owl, to which Pooh replied that Everyone was perfectly happy to share, unlike a certain Someone who was after Eeyore's thistles, which was why they had come to see him.

'In that case, you had better come in,' said Owl.

Owl's table was very grand but by the time Pooh, Piglet, Rabbit, Kanga and Eeyore had sat down, there were no chairs for Rabbit's friends and relations, so they made themselves at home under the table and talked among themselves.

'Given that it's Eeyore's problem, I will address him,' said Owl, hoping to speed things up.

'Eeyore doesn't need addressing, Owl,' said Pooh. 'We know where he lives.'

'Yet you hardly ever visit,' complained Eeyore.

Owl, who was rather wishing he'd pretended he wasn't in, explained that by addressing Eeyore, he simply wanted to ask him what was wrong.

'Thank you for caring, Owl,' said Eeyore. 'But I have such a long list of What Is Wrong, I don't know where to start ...'

'There's Another Donkey,' said Pooh, in case Eeyore didn't know when to stop.

'Possibly three,' added Piglet.

Owl shut his eyes and counted to ten while he thought of a sensible thing to ask.

'It would help with my enquiries,' he said, 'if someone could tell me what the animal in question looked like.'

'Show him, Pooh!' said Piglet.

Pooh waited until Piglet had shut his eyes and pulled the face of Another Donkey. Owl almost fell off his chair, but after Kanga had helped him back up, he said: 'Excuse me for stating the obvious, but that looks like Eeyore, only smiling.'

'Which Eeyore never does,' said Pooh, 'so it must be Another Donkey.'

Owl thought about this while Kanga poured the tea, saying things like 'Not necessarily so!' and 'What's the likelihood?', then he turned to Eeyore and said: 'Is it an indisputable fact that your countenance is always one of gloom?'

Eeyore stared at him blankly.

'Do you ever smile?' said Owl.

Eeyore thought hard and then he remembered.

'I might have done this morning when I found a new patch of thistles, but when I went to eat them, I saw Another Donkey in the pond.'

'What was it doing there?' asked Owl.

'Looking far too pleased for my liking!' said Eeyore.

Owl nodded knowingly.

'I put it to you, my friend,' he said, 'that what you saw was not Another Donkey, but your own reflection.'

'Ah,' said Pooh, who often did his stoutness exercises in front of a mirror. Eeyore looked pitifully at Owl, then Piglet, then Pooh.

'If only that was true ...' he said, 'but I know my own reflection when I see it and what I saw looked like Another Donkey altogether.'

'If you don't believe me, try looking at yourself in the teapot,' said Owl, giving it an extra polish.

'Is it a Party Game?' said Eeyore. 'Only I'm not in the mood.'

Owl put the teapot in front of him.

'Oh well, if you insist,' grumbled Eeyore.

He glanced at his face in the shiny surface.

'That's me all right,' he said. 'I'd know that sad

expression anywhere.'

'Look closer,' said Owl.

This time when Eeyore looked,
the round teapot made his face look
so funny, he broke into a big smile,
which made Piglet gasp and even Owl
flapped his wings nervously.

'See?' he cried. 'There's Another
Donkey! It's following me!'

'It's *you*, dear!' said Kanga.
'That's how you look when
you're happy.'

'Is it?' said Eeyore.

He leant towards the teapot and
smiled again just to make sure.

'And it was just my own
reflection in the pond?'

Everybody nodded and
seeing that it was him after
all, Eeyore smiled and smiled
and he was still smiling when
Pooh left to tell Tigger that he
could stop minding the thistles, because there never was
Another Donkey like Eeyore.

Summer

in which Pooh dreams of the Sauce of the Nile

BY

KATE SAUNDERS

ONE VERY SUNNY MORNING, POOH AND PIGLET were sitting outside Pooh's house in a warm patch of shade.

'I wonder,' said Pooh. 'If Africa is as hot as this?'

Piglet was idly sorting his haycorns into piles of small, medium and large. The heat made his head feel pleasantly fuzzy. 'What's that, Pooh?'

'I was just thinking about Africa,' said Pooh. 'In particular, the Sauce of the Nile.'

Piglet was puzzled. 'The what?'

Pooh wasn't exactly sure. He rested his paws on his knees, which was a good thinking position, and was quiet for such a long time that a large white butterfly settled on one of his ears for a rest.

'Well, Piglet,' he said at last, 'Christopher Robin read me a bit of his book about the Nile last night. It's a very long river in Africa, and some explorers went there to look for the Sauce.'

'Oh,' said Piglet. 'Did they find it?'

'I think so,' said Pooh. 'I was very sleepy when Christopher Robin read that bit.'

'What did it look like?'

'I was asleep by then,' said Pooh. 'But Christopher Robin says all rivers have a Sauce. He says explorers follow rivers right back to where they start – and they know it's the start because there's the Sauce. It might be apple sauce.'

Piglet was now very confused. 'In a jug, Pooh?'

'I expect so,' said Pooh. 'A jug, or perhaps a bowl.'

'Oh,' said Piglet politely. The sun was getting warmer every minute, the air was filled with the drowsy humming of insects, and he felt too hot and lazy to bother about sauce.

'I know this isn't Africa,' Pooh went on. 'But there IS a river here, Piglet – and if there's a river, that makes me feel there must be Sauce. Don't you feel it too?'

Piglet didn't, but said, 'Where do you think it might be, Pooh?'

'It's quite simple,' said Pooh, standing up and licking a stray smear of honey off one paw. 'We'll go to the river to find out where it's coming from, and when we find the Sauce, we can eat it.'

Piglet, who was quite happy where he was, said, 'Yes, we must do that one day.'

But the idea had stuck in Pooh's brain and wouldn't go away. 'We'll take plenty of

supplies for the journey,' he went on, as if Piglet hadn't said anything. 'I'll pack a jar of honey.'

'I suppose I could take a few of my haycorns,' Piglet said, cheering up – for there was something summery and holiday-ish about setting off for an adventure on a bright morning.

The Forest was filled with the sights, sounds and smells of a hot summer's day – there were canopies of green leaves, dazzling in the sunlight, prickly bushes of wild roses that hummed with bees, and spiderwebs covered with glittering silver dew.

They had only been walking for a short while when, along the woodland path, came Rabbit carrying a shopping basket over one arm.

'Hullo, Rabbit,' said Pooh.

'Hullo, Pooh and Piglet,' said Rabbit. 'Where are you two off to?'

'We're looking for the Sauce of the river,' Piglet explained. 'Which is like the Sauce they found in the Nile.'

'Oh, that,' said Rabbit, who never liked admitting he didn't know something.

'Have you ever seen it, Rabbit?' asked Pooh.

'Hundreds of times,' said Rabbit carelessly. 'I'd come with you, but you'll never get there before nightfall. And I don't fancy being lost in a dark forest full of angry Heffalumps.'

The word 'Heffalumps' struck terror into Piglet, though he tried to look brave and don't-carish. 'Oh ... r-really?' he squeaked, 'Why are they angry?'

Rabbit shrugged. 'Probably because you dug that trap for them.' He liked it even less when people asked questions about things he'd made up to hide not knowing.

'Well now,' Pooh said thoughtfully, 'Christopher Robin did mention that there were Heffalumps in Africa ... perhaps they hang about near the Sauce of every river. If we meet one, we'll just explain that we didn't mean any harm.'

'Hmm, yes, I suppose you could try that,' said Rabbit. 'I suppose you *might* meet one who isn't as angry as the others. Personally, I wouldn't risk it.'

'Oh, help!' gasped Piglet, not even pretending to be brave any more.

'Anyway, I must be getting along,' said Rabbit. 'Good morning.'

And he disappeared into the darkest part of the Forest, where the leaves were thickest.

'Pooh,' quavered Piglet, 'I've just remembered something I forgot to do and I can only do it if I go home.'

'No, Piglet,' Pooh said firmly. 'If Rabbit's seen the Sauce, that means we must be getting closer.'

'All right,' said Piglet in a wobbly voice, not really feeling all right at all.

They began walking again, along the winding path that went through the Six Pine Trees towards the river.

'Pooh,' said Piglet, after a long silence, 'I'm worried that if we meet a Heffalump, we won't have time to explain anything.'

Pooh stopped walking and rubbed his head with his paw, which was a sign that he was thinking particularly hard.

'We'll probably hear it rustling in the bushes before it jumps out at us,' he said slowly. 'And that would be the time to shout something at it.'

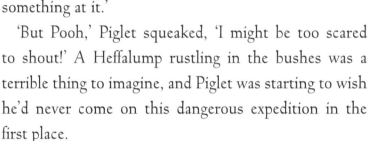

'But Pooh,' Piglet squeaked, 'I might be too scared to shout!' A Heffalump rustling in the bushes was a terrible thing to imagine, and Piglet was starting to wish he'd never come on this dangerous expedition in the first place.

'Leave it to me,' said Pooh. 'If I hear any rustling, I'll shout something like, "Stop! Pooh and Piglet didn't mean any harm with the Heffalump trap!"'

Piglet was doubtful. 'What if it doesn't listen?'

'Hmm,' said Pooh. 'Maybe we should shout something *before* we hear rustling – I'll think of something that sounds polite.' He began stomping along the path again, and Piglet trotted beside him, thinking that it was very dark under the pine trees and a polite shout would be better than nothing.

'I know,' said Pooh. 'We should talk very loudly about how much we *like* Heffalumps. They won't attack us if we're saying nice things about them.' In a louder voice, he said, 'Oh I *do* like Heffalumps! Aren't they *kind*, Piglet? Don't you think Heffalumps are *handsome?*'

Pooh marched along the path, shouting out nice things about Heffalumps, and Piglet helped by sometimes shouting, 'Yes!', and in a very short time they came out of the deep shade of the pine trees into a sunlit clearing.

'It worked,' Pooh said, with great satisfaction. 'Not a Heffalump in sight!'

'Well done, Pooh,' said Piglet. They only had to walk a little further and there was the river – which was so slow and sleepy in the heat that Pooh and Piglet had to stare at it for a few minutes to work out which way it was flowing. When they had decided, they set off along the bank towards the Sauce.

All of a sudden they heard splashing and shrieking, and when they turned round a bend in the stream, they found Kanga and Roo. Kanga was sitting on the bank, watching Roo while he played in the shallow water.

'Hooray, it's Pooh and Piglet!' shouted Roo. 'Look at me splashing, Pooh! Look at the big splashes I make when I jump, Piglet!'

'Try to stay out of the mud, dear,' said Kanga. 'Hullo, you two; I was just unpacking my picnic basket.'

The words 'picnic' and 'basket' reminded Pooh that it was a long time since breakfast. He said, 'Hullo, Kanga,' and went over to

look at the things she was taking out of her big basket. There was a red-and-white cloth to spread on the ground, some sandwiches wrapped in paper, a little pot of Roo-food and several interesting jars that made Pooh think about lunch.

Kanga saw that Pooh was looming over her in an Interested way, and kindly said, 'Why don't you join us?'

'Thank you, Kanga,' said Pooh. 'I was hoping to have the Sauce for lunch, but it can wait; it might even be nicer at teatime.'

'What sauce is that, dear?' Kanga asked.

Pooh and Piglet sat down beside her and explained about the Sauce of the Nile. And while they were explaining, Pooh ate his jar of honey and Kanga's tin

of condensed milk, and Piglet ate all his haycorns. It was very pleasant to sit in the shade, watching the lazy progress of the river, and Piglet began to think that the journey to the Sauce could be put off until another day when it wasn't so hot.

But Kanga said, 'I'd like to see this sauce. If it's apple sauce, it'll do very nicely for Roo's tea.'

'We don't know what sort it is,' said Piglet. 'It might be the Wrong Sort.'

Kanga didn't hear him because she had noticed that Roo was playing with his food and keeping it all in his mouth instead of swallowing it, until his cheeks were puffed out. 'Do stop that, dear.'

'Mmmm!' said Roo. He swallowed his mouthful of food in a hurry, and said, 'What about Tigger?'

'Oh, I haven't forgotten Tigger,' said Kanga. 'I just wanted to save our lunch from too much bouncing.'

She took from her basket a large bottle of Roo's Extract of Malt (which had turned out to be what Tiggers like to eat), and called out, 'Tigger, dear ... lunchtime!'

If Piglet hadn't known it was Tigger, he might have mistaken the sounds of his approach for a whole herd of rampaging Heffalumps. The excitable animal came crashing towards them through the leaves, snapping twigs and alarming some of Rabbit's smaller friends

and relations in the undergrowth.

'Hullopoohandpiglet. Phew – it's too hot for Tiggers today!' said Tigger breathlessly, as he flung himself across the picnic cloth (luckily Kanga had cleared away what was left of the food). 'You shouldn't bounce so much, dear,' said Kanga, giving him the bottle of malt. 'It can't be good for your digestion.'

Tigger slurped his Extract of Malt and Kanga and Pooh told him about the journey they were about to take to find the Sauce of the river.

'I think I've just been there,' said Tigger. 'I was going along the bit of the river that's closest to Christopher Robin's house when I saw it.'

Pooh asked, 'Saw what?'

'The Sauce,' said Tigger. 'There it was, in the middle of a big tree stump.'

Pooh and Piglet were so excited to hear this that Pooh forgot the last lick of condensed milk and Piglet stopped not wanting to carry on with the journey.

'I knew we were getting closer,' Pooh said happily. 'What did it look like, Tigger?'

'A bit like that,' said Tigger – and he pointed his paw at Pooh's empty jar of honey.

'Now, Tigger dear,' said Kanga. 'Are you sure that's what you saw? Were you the right way up when you looked at it?'

'Yes!' said Tigger, with an impatient bounce. 'It was just like that!'

'So the Sauce looks like honey,' Pooh said, rubbing his head. 'Did you happen to taste it?'

'No,' said Tigger. 'Tiggers don't like honey, or anything that looks like it might be honey.'

'Perhaps it's something nice for tea,' said Kanga. 'Come along, Roo.'

Pooh and Piglet, Kanga and Roo and Tigger began to walk (or bounce) along the river bank, until they came

to the place that was closest to Christopher Robin's house.

Tigger and Roo bounced eagerly towards the tree stump where Tigger had seen the Sauce.

'Found it!' Tigger's voice shouted back at the others. 'It still looks like a jar of honey!'

Pooh was very pleased to hear that the Sauce of the river was so much like honey, but he was also puzzled. 'I wonder why I've never noticed it before.'

'This doesn't look like the beginning of the river,' said Piglet. 'Or the end. We're still in the middle. So that can't be the proper Sauce.'

'Hmm,' said Pooh. 'I'd better taste it, to make sure there's nothing the matter with it.' He hurried towards the large, flat tree stump.

'And there's bread and jam now!' said Roo, happily.

To the amazement of Pooh and Piglet, the tree stump was spread not only with a large jar marked 'HONEY',

but also a loaf of bread, a pot of strawberry jam and a heap of little spoons.

'How thoughtful,' said Kanga.

Pooh had to rub his head with his paw for a long time to make sense of it all.

Piglet asked, 'Was there anything about honey and bread and jam in that book about the Sauce of the Nile, Pooh?'

'No,' said Pooh slowly. 'But that doesn't mean it wasn't there.'

At that moment, the door of Christopher Robin's house opened, and out came Christopher Robin himself, carrying a large tray.

Everyone ran to hug him, taking care not to make him drop the tray.

'It's such a lovely day that I decided to have a tea party for all my friends,' said Christopher Robin. 'I've nearly finished laying the table and I was just going to come and look for you all. What are you doing here?'

'We're looking for the Sauce of the river,' explained Pooh. 'Like the Sauce of the Nile.'

'We thought it might be like apple sauce,' said Piglet. 'And in a jug.'

'Oh,' said Christopher Robin. He put down the tray.

'I think you might be a bit mixed-up, Pooh. Some words like to be in two places at once and not mean the same thing at all.'

'What words?' asked Pooh.

Christopher Robin thought hard for a moment, then said, 'Well, RAW food, which isn't cooked, hardly ever ROARS. And the book I read to you last night was about the SOURCE of the Nile, which means the beginning, and you eat apple SAUCE near the end.'

'Oh!' said Pooh.

'OH!' said everyone.

Piglet felt a little silly, until Christopher Robin said, 'How clever of you to come to my tea party before I even invited you,' which made it much better.

'I *knew* I'd end up with something nice to eat,' said Pooh happily. 'And I'm glad it's honey and not sauce.'

It wasn't time for tea yet. Christopher Robin sent Tigger off to tell Owl, Eeyore, Rabbit and all their friends about the party, including any of Rabbit's friends and relations who happened to be in the area (some of them were too small to travel long distances).

While they were waiting for everyone to arrive, Pooh and Christopher Robin sat side by side in a shady place,

leaning against the trunk of a big tree.

'You're very quiet, Pooh,' said Christopher Robin.

'That's because I'm thinking,' said Pooh. 'And I can't think and talk at the same time.'

'What are you thinking about?'

'I was trying to think of something nicer than a summer tea party,' said Pooh. 'But I can't, because there isn't anything nicer. Now I've got that settled, I think I'll stop thinking.' He folded his paws on his round stomach and gazed at the tea table with a look of dreamy contentment.

And Christopher Robin smiled, and said to himself, 'Dear old bear!'

AFTERWORD

PAUL BRIGHT

I have, somewhere on my bookshelf, a copy of *Winnie-the-Pooh* in Latin, called *Winnie Ille Pu*, which shows Pooh wearing a Roman helmet. I may have had that picture at the back of my mind when Eeyore found the Something Interesting. My dragon, even though he never appears, is, I think, a close relative of the dragon that Christopher Robin talks to in the poem 'In the Dark', from *Now We Are Six*. And then there is Piglet. Piglet is very small and very shy, but he is also cleverer than some of the other creatures realise. In *Winnie-the-Pooh*, when Piglet was surrounded by water, he wrote a message saying: 'HELP! PIGLIT (ME)', and I thought he might like to do some more writing this time. And he thought so too.

BRIAN SIBLEY

I have loved A.A.Milne's stories and poems (and E.H.Shepard's pictures that go with them) since I was very young. Later, when I was rather older, I had the pleasure of getting to know Christopher Robin Milne, corresponding with Ernest Shepard and writing about their history with that 'Bear of Little Brain' in my book *Three Cheers for Pooh!*

The idea for my story came from seeing an old photograph showing Milne and the young Christopher Robin playing with Winnie-the-Pooh – *and* a toy penguin!

Just supposing, I thought, that Penguin, like Kanga, Roo and Tigger, had, one day, found his way into the Hundred Acre Wood …

A.A.Milne and his son,
Christopher Robin, playing with
Winnie-the-Pooh and Penguin.

JEANNE WILLIS

Why was I so thrilled and delighted to contribute to this anthology? To quote Christopher Robin, 'Wherever I am, there's always Pooh, there's always Pooh and me.' It has been that way since my Auntie Kay gave me a copy of *When We Were Very Young* for my fifth birthday. That same year, I starred as the queen in the Wheatfields Infants' School production of 'The King's Breakfast' and apart from my melodramatic gagging when the 'king' attempted to kiss me in the manner suggested in the poem, it was one of my finest moments.

Pooh is with me still and always will be. He filled my childhood days with sunshine, even when it rained and rained and rained. But more than that, he was my muse and a very amusing muse he was too. He inspired the rhythm for my own writing and, for that, I am eternally grateful, so ... three cheers for Pooh! (For who?) For Pooh!

KATE SAUNDERS

Pooh and I go back a long way. One of my earliest memories is of my father reading the stories to us, and weaving Pooh references into everyday life – for instance, one of our favourite outings was called 'stopping for a Little Something', which usually meant Coke and crisps in a pub garden. Dad taught me to appreciate Pooh's talent for simply sitting in the moment and enjoying life, and I have always loved the old bear's

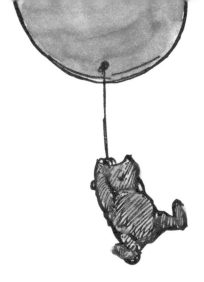

unfailing optimism; he is a blue-skies sort of bear, and that was the spirit I tried to get into my story. Some of his ideas might be on the silly side, but no matter what happens, he is always delighted and never disappointed – in the Hundred Acre Wood, all endings are happy.

MARK BURGESS

I was delighted to be asked to illustrate this new collection of Winnie-the-Pooh stories. The idea of having four stories set throughout the year was particularly attractive to me, as I love the different seasons. It was a lovely opportunity to show the

Forest in all its variety. And, of course, I relished the chance to draw Pooh and his friends – both old and new. They are so much fun to be with and the authors of this book have given them some wonderful new adventures.

About A.A.Milne

A.A.Milne was born in London in 1882. He began his writing career with humorous pieces for *Punch* magazine. It was in this publication, in 1923, that Winnie-the-Pooh made his first appearance in the poem 'Teddy Bear'. Milne also wrote plays and by the time his first book of poems *When We Were Very Young*, was published in 1924, he had already made his name as a dramatist and novelist.

About E.H.Shepard

E.H.Shepard was born in 1879 and became known as the 'Man who drew Pooh'. But he was also an acclaimed artist in his own right. Shepard won

a scholarship to the Royal Academy Schools, and much later, worked for *Punch* magazine as a cartoonist and illustrator. Shepard's illustrations of Winnie-the-Pooh and the friends of the Hundred Acre Wood have become classics in their own right and are recognised all over the world.